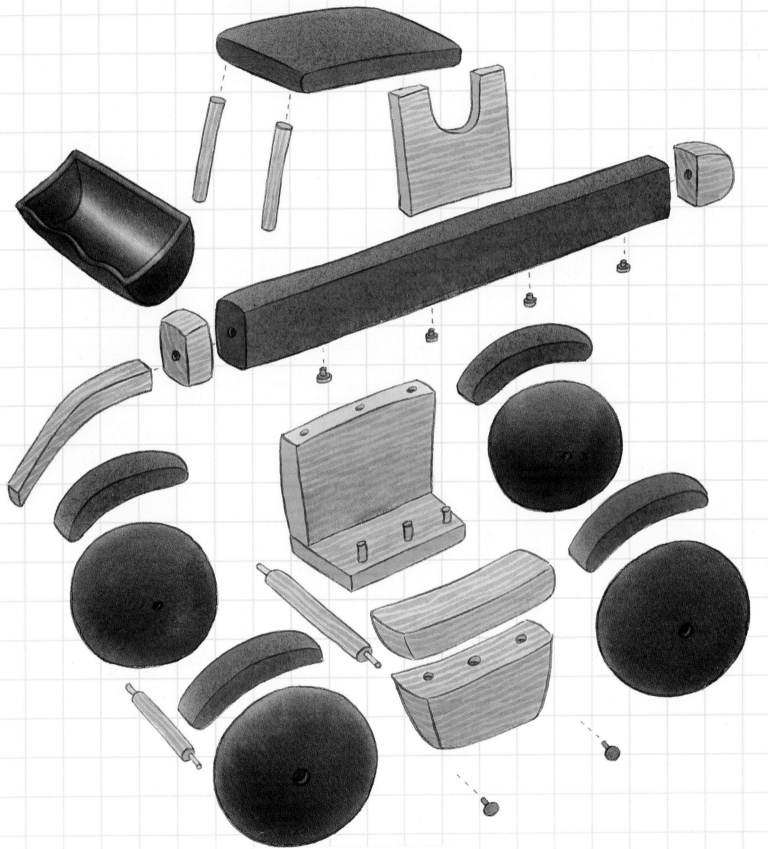

TELESCOPIC HANDLER

For Luka, Monika and Teddy Traynor and for Joseph Cyril Bamforth,
the big JCB in the sky.

The Flying Diggers

Ian Whybrow and David Melling

First published in 2009 by Hodder Children's Books

Text copyright © Ian Whybrow 2009
Illustration copyright © David Melling 2009

Hodder Children's Books
338 Euston Road
London NW1 3BH

Hodder Children's Books Australia
Level 17/207 Kent Street
Sydney, NSW 2000

A catalogue record of this book is available
from the British Library.

ISBN: 978 0 340 90312 4
10 9 8 7 6 5 4 3 2 1

Printed in China

Hodder Children's Books
is a division of Hachette
Children's Books.
An Hachette UK Company.
www.hachette.co.uk

The Flying Diggers

Ian Whybrow
and
David Melling

Hodder
Children's
Books

A division of Hachette Children's Books

Teddy was in Granbam's garden when Ruby came
round to play.
Granbam was in his workshop.
"What does your Granbam
do in there?" asked Ruby.

"He makes things," said Teddy.

"Are these diggers any good to you?" asked Granbam. "I've just finished them."

"Wow!" said Teddy. "I think this orange one is a BACKHOE LOADER."

"And the blue one is a TELESCOPIC HANDLER!" said Ruby. "Thanks, Granbam!" they said together.

"You'll need these hard hats and keys,"
said Granbam. "Hang onto them.
They're a bit spesh."
"What's special about them?" asked Teddy.
"Aha!" smiled Granbam. "That's for you
to find out."

The children were busy giving the diggers a go,
when suddenly their keys went Flash! Flash!
And a voice came in through their hard hats,

"Calling **TEAM FD!**

Calling **TEAM FD!**

EMERGENCY!

Tiger cub in DANGER!

Hurry to the jungle,

TEAM FD!"

"Who's Team FD?" said Ruby.

"That's us!" said Teddy. "F is for Flying, D's for Diggers.

I'll take the orange backhoe loader and you take

the blue telescopic handler!

Put in your special key and let's go!"

They went…

"1-2-3 to turn the key. 4 to get inside!

ACTION STATIONS!

TEAM FD!

TIME TO TAKE A RIDE!"

The engines roared and up they soared.
Over the garden, over the park, higher
than clouds. Far away they flew till they
saw the jungle miles below.

"Mind out for those parrots!" called Ruby.
"Whee! I love it up here!"

"Me, too!" called Teddy. "Let's hope we're not too late!"

Then Teddy caught a glimpse of something bright and stripy.

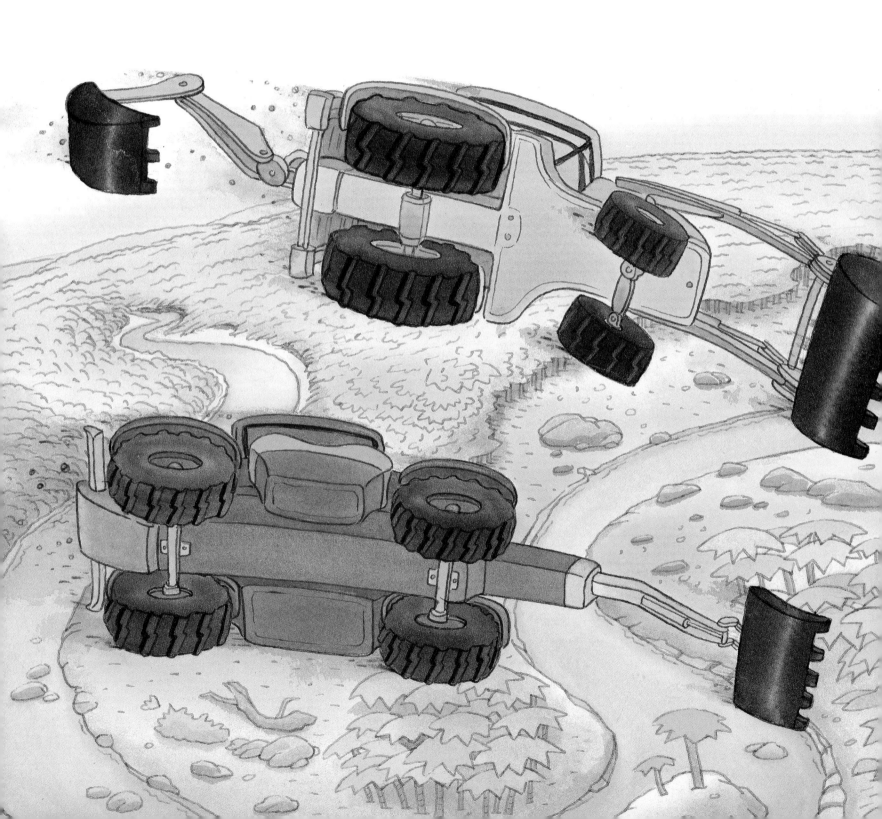

"Tiger, tiger by the river!" he called.
"Stand by to nosedive, Ruby!"
"3-2-1, dive-bomb!" yelled Ruby,
and down they thundered, deep into
the steamy green jungle.

The tiger cub was just clinging on... his claws
were starting to slip... his tail was dangling down...

and the crocodiles' teeth were getting closer
with every **snap-snap!**

"You save the tiger cub and leave the crocodiles to me!" ordered Teddy.

So Ruby sent out her telescopic arm and up went the tiger cub.

Whoosh!

Down came Teddy's front
loader and scooped up
a bucketful of crocodiles.

In two ticks, the tiger cub was back
with his mother.
"Good work, Ruby!"
Then it was time to deal with those snappy
old crocodiles!
Teddy pulled the lever and tipped them
back into the river with a mighty…

....splosh!

"Job done!" said Ruby and Teddy.
"Let's get back to base."
The engines roared and up they soared,
racing through the skies.
Higher than birds, higher than clouds,
and back to Granbam's garden.

The moment they
landed, they said
the last part together,

"1-2-3,
Take out your key –
You deserve a rest.
Well done, Flying Diggers,
You are just the BEST!"

"Hello you two!" smiled Granbam.

"So what do you think of my little diggers?"

"A bit spesh!" said Teddy and Ruby together.

"What are you going
to make for us next,
Granbam?"

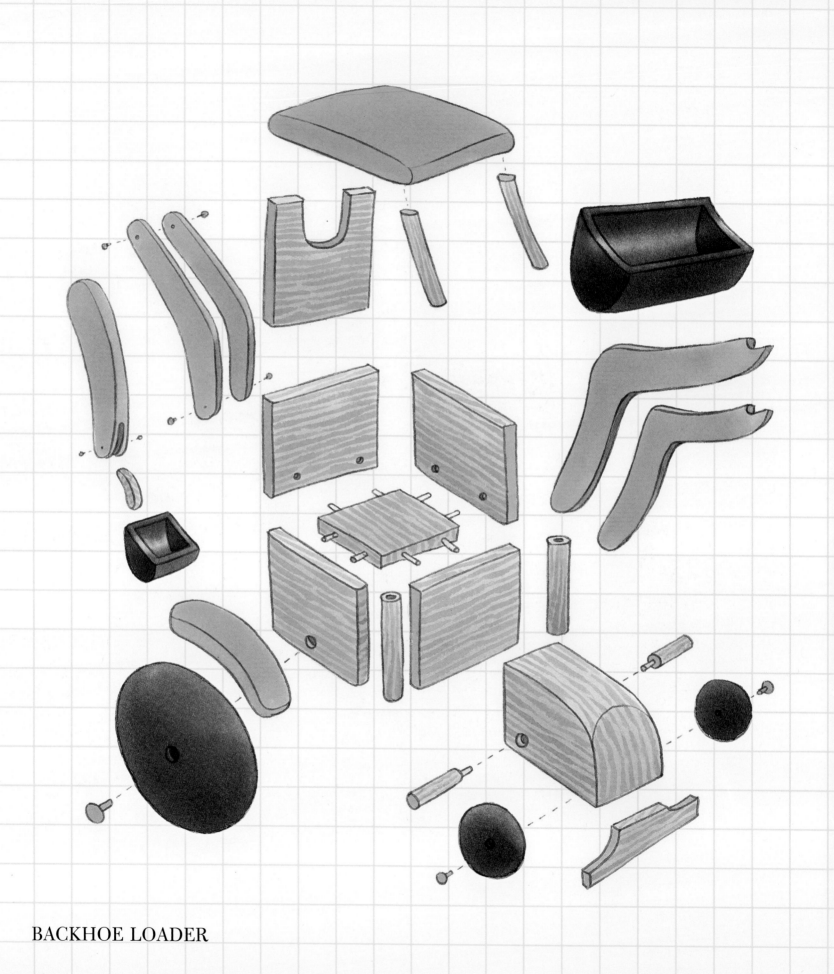

BACKHOE LOADER